D0363866

For Tom, Diana, Alex and Amy
with lots of love from Embo xxx

Bloomsbury Publishing, London, Oxford, New York, New Delhi and Sydney

First published in Great Britain in 2018 by Bloomsbury Publishing Plc
50 Bedford Square, London WC1B 3DP

www.bloomsbury.com

BLOOMSBURY is a registered trademark of Bloomsbury Publishing Plc

Text and illustrations copyright © Emily MacKenzie 2018
The moral rights of the author/illustrator have been asserted

All rights reserved
No part of this publication may be reproduced or
transmitted by any means, electronic, mechanical, photocopying
or otherwise, without the prior permission of the publisher

A CIP catalogue record of this book is available from the British Library

ISBN 978 1 4088 7400 4 (HB)
ISBN 978 1 4088 8296 2 (PB)
ISBN 978 1 4088 8294 8 (eBook)

All papers used by Bloomsbury Publishing are natural, recyclable products made
from wood grown in well managed forests. The manufacturing processes
conform to the environmental regulations of the country of origin

Printed in China by Leo Paper Products, Heshan, Guangdong
1 3 5 7 9 10 8 6 4 2

Eric Makes a SPLASH.

Emily MacKenzie

BLOOMSBURY
LONDON OXFORD NEW YORK NEW DELHI SYDNEY

Eric was a **worrier**.

He **worried** about **noises** in the **night**.

He **worried** about finding
spiders in his **welly boots**.

He **worried** about
getting **lost** at the **park**.

But nothing worried Eric more than . . .

"no thanks."

. . . trying NEW things.

"hmmm..."

"eek!"

Luckily Eric had a **brave** and **kind** best friend
who **loved** to help him feel **brave** too.

Flora was **fearless** and Eric thought she was just **wonderful!**

On Monday Flora wanted to **splash** in **muddy puddles** but Eric worried about getting his boots dirty.

"Why don't you pretend you're a **piglet** rolling in mud or a **hippo** having a bath?" suggested Flora.

Soon they were

sploshing
and
splashing
together.

"Ta-dah!" said Flora. "Look! A swimming cap with a **dinosaur** on it. This will keep your fur dry.

And how about these goggles?"

But Eric **still** worried. Until ...

"Now we're getting somewhere!"
said Eric with a smile.

Finally they were off to the pool.

Everyone jumped in!

But Eric just sat on the side.

SPLOSH

"Why don't you pretend you're a **dolphin**,
or a seal, or a **shark**, or a **turtle**?" said Flora.
"They're all GREAT at **swimming**!"

But this time the idea of pretending to be
something else **didn't** make Eric feel braver.

So after a few **very** deep,
very brave breaths,
Flora and Eric held hands,
counted to three

1
2
3

and . . .

SWOOSH!

SWISH!

SLIPPY!

SLIDEY!

SPLISH!

SPLOSH!

SPLASH!

. . . They made it **all** the way to the bottom TOGETHER!
"Because best friends are **always** there
when you need them," smiled Eric.

good morning

hello

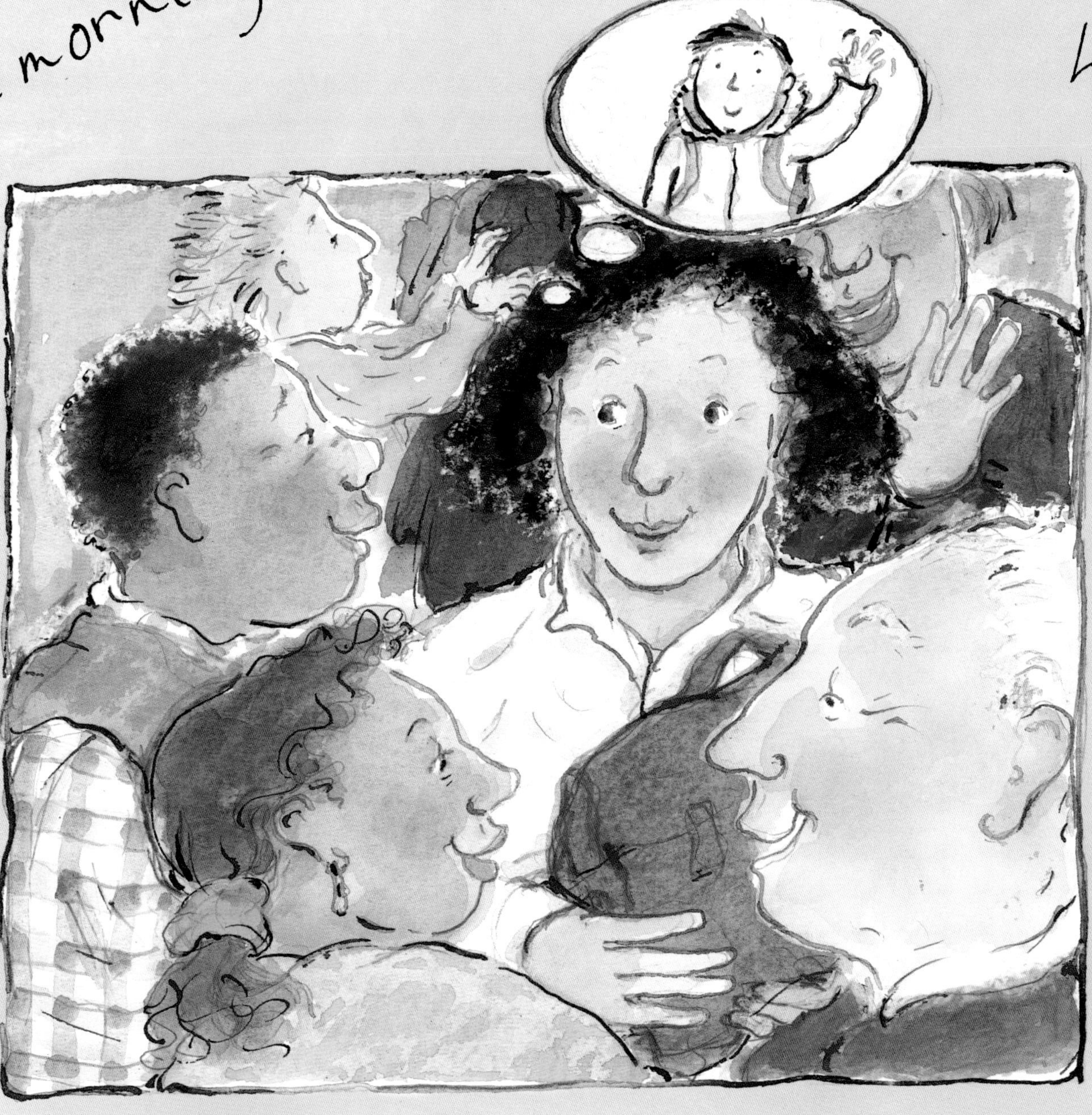

hello Bella

hi Sam!

Then we had biscuits with chocolate chips in them, and a drink.

Then it was time to put our
sports shoes on and run around.

I sat down and tried hard to do
my very best writing.

I had my sandwiches for lunch, and
I thought about you all the time
I was eating them.

After lunch I was sleepy,
but there was lots more to do.

With all the things we'd done,
there was quite a mess to clear up!

Then there was a story. It was funny – I laughed and laughed.

At home time, I put on my
coat and thought about you.

I held your hand all the way home.
What have you been doing today?